For Nick Dewar,
whose doodles were always better than mine

Library of Congress Cataloging-in-Publication Data

Collins, Ross.
Doodleday / Ross Collins.
p. cm.
ISBN 978-0-8075-1683-6
[1. Drawing—Fiction. 2. Mothers and sons—Fiction.] I. Title.
PZ7.C6836Doo 2011
[E]—dc22
2010031128

10 9 8 7 6 5 4 3 2 BP 15 14 13

For more information about Albert Whitman & Company,
please visit our web site at www.albertwhitman.com

SUNDA

25
30 31

"I'm going to the store now," said Harvey's mom.
"Don't bother your dad—he's tied up with work."
"Fine," said Harvey. "I'll just do some drawing."

NG?"

shrieked Mom, snatching the pencil from Harvey's hand.

"DRAWING…
on Doodleday?
Are you crazy?"

"What's **Doodleday?**" asked Harvey.

"NOBODY
draws on
Doodleday
and that's that!"

"Why does…" Harvey began, but Mom was already gone.

As soon as Mom was out of sight, Harvey took
out the pencils he kept in his secret shoebox.
"Doodleday indeed," thought Harvey.
He'd never heard of such nonsense.
One small drawing couldn't hurt a fly.

"That's it," thought Harvey.

"I'll draw a fly."

It was an excellent fly.

Fat...

and hairy

and...

What was that noise in the kitchen?

"**My fly!**" gasped Harvey.
Harvey's fly was fat, hairy, and **ENORMOUS**,
and it was **destroying the kitchen**.
Harvey was worried—
no fly swatter would work on this monster.
"What gets rid of flies?" he thought. "Spiders! That's it!
Spiders eat flies for breakfast!"

Harvey ran back to the living room
and quickly drew a big, hairy spider.

But **Harvey's spider**
didn't care for flies.
It was far more interested
in his dad.

Harvey wondered if
a drawing could eat you.
He wasn't going to wait to find out…

"What eats spiders? Birds! That's it! Birds love eating spiders!"
Harvey drew a great big bird, with talons and a big, bug-munching beak.

As soon as Harvey finished drawing, he heard a terrifying

SQUAWK!

from outside.

There above the house was **Harvey's bird.**

And there was Mr. Bagshaw's fence,

being turned into a nest.

Mr. Bagshaw wasn't happy at all…

… and neither were the other neighbors.

"Are these your drawings, Harvey?"

"Don't you know it's
Doodleday?"

"You fix this RIGHT NOW, young man!"

"**Huge,**" thought Harvey.
"Only something **huge**
could reach up there."

Harvey grabbed his pad and drew
the biggest creature in the world…

The giant squid decided to
DESTROY the STREET.

"**Mom!**" cried Harvey...

"What were you thinking, Harvey?" yelled Mom.
"It's Doodleday!"
"I didn't mean to!" cried Harvey.
Mom grabbed the pad and started to scribble furiously.

Harvey couldn't see what she was drawing.
What could **swat** a giant fly?
Eat a gigantic spider?
Bring down a monstrous bird?
Be **more ferocious** than a giant squid?

Mom drew...

Mom! Doodle Mom walked calmly up the street, gave a little cough, and bellowed...

ALL RIGHT, YOU FOUR— GET BACK IN THAT PAD OR ELSE!

Mom held open the pad.

In buzzed the **fly**.

In crawled the **spider**.

In flew the **bird**.

In squeezed the **squid**.

"Thank you kindly," said Mom.
"My pleasure," said Doodle Mom.
She shook Mom's hand politely and stepped inside.

With a SNAP, the pad was shut.

Harvey's mom scratched her head and sighed.
"Now help me get your father
down from that lamppost."

"Is Doodleday every year?"

asked Harvey.